BUG BLONSKY

and His Swamp Scout Survival Guide

E. S. REDMOND

CANDLEWICK PRESS

x

First edition 2021

Library of Congress Catalog Card Number pending
ISBN 978-1-5362-0676-0

21 22 23 24 25 26 LEO 10 9 8 7 6 5 4 3 2 1

Printed in Heshan, Guangdong, China

This book was typeset in Chaparral and Bokka.
The illustrations were done in pen and ink and watercolor.

Candlewick Press
99 Dover Street
Somerville, Massachusetts 02144

www.candlewick.com

For my mother, Judy,
who has never stopped believing in me

Abner Vanderpelt has six merit patches on his Swamp Scout vest already. I have three. OK, fine, I only have two—the yellow one is just a mustard stain I got while eating a hot dog.

Our troop was supposed to earn a bunch of merit patches during our overnight trip to Camp Win-Kee-Noo this weekend, but it

looks like the only patches I'll be going home with are red and itchy ones from poison ivy since Mrs. V. is almost done handing them out and still hasn't called my name. Mrs. V. is our troop's "marsh mother," but she also happens to be Abner's *real* mother, which sorta stinks because it's been like having *two* of him around all weekend, except one wears pink lipstick and too much perfume.

It also stinks because in order to earn the patches Mrs. V. chose, you have to be really good at stuff like "paying attention" and "following directions," which I'm not.

There are hardly any patches for stuff I'm good at. If there were, I'd probably have even more patches than Abner by now.

STUFF I'M SUPER GOOD AT

messiness
(yellow mustard stain)

Being Loud

Armpit Farting

Daydreaming

Being Wiggly

Playing Video Games

Paper Airplane
construction

Being a True
Bigfoot Believer

Staying Up
Past Bedtime

Forgetting Things patch
would go here if I could
remember where I left it.

The only patch I really cared about earning was the Curious Creature patch for spotting an odd or uncommon animal, but even though I spent this *whole entire* weekend looking, I never found Bigfoot, who I know for sure is totally 100 percent real, even if no one believes me.

Abner kept insisting with that know-it-all look on his face that if Bigfoot were real, he would be listed in the "Terrible Things to Avoid" section of our Swamp Scout survival guide, but I don't think that proves anything because Abner is real and he isn't listed in that section either.

In fact, I learned tons of stuff this weekend that should be listed in the survival guide and isn't, so I decided to write my own.

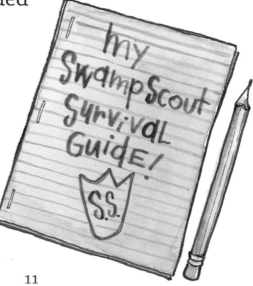

1. Only discuss Bigfoot with TBBs (True Bigfoot Believers).

Because if you happen to be at a Swamp Scout meeting when you tell your best friend, Louie, all the cool and interesting facts you learned by reading Bigfoot's autobiography, Abner will butt in and tell Louie that you're full of baloney because Bigfoot is only a myth.

Then Kirby Dinklage will laugh and tell the whole troop that only a baby first-grader would believe that Bigfoot is real. And even though the last thing you'd ever want to do is spend a weekend with Abner and Kirby, you'll be the first one to sign up for the Swamp Scout camping trip just for a chance to prove them wrong.

2. Bring a handkerchief.

Because when your mom drops you at the bus, she will get all emotional since this is your first overnight and she will keep telling you what a "Big Bug" you are and that she's so proud of you. Then she will kiss you too many times and leave smooches all over your face, and you'll bet no one else's mom would ever be so totally embarrassing.

3. Keep your trail map in your pocket.

Because if you take it out to look at it, you'll end up folding it into a super-duper double-looper airplane. Then Louie will want to see it fly, and you will too, so you'll throw it down the bus aisle.

Then on its second loop-de-loop, it will smack Abner square in the back of his head, and he will think you did it on purpose, and before you can explain that it was just an accident, he will have already told on you.

4. Pretend to listen by nodding a lot.

That way, when Mrs. V. comes over and does that thing grown-ups do where they bend down to look you in the eye and put their face *way* too close to yours while talking very softly about your behavior, she'll *think* you are listening and agreeing with her when really you're just thinking that she has pink lipstick on her teeth.

5. Go to the bathroom before the bus ride.

Because even though you really didn't have to go before you got on the bus, you *really will* have to go after a while *just like Mom said*, and it will be super hard to concentrate on beating Louie at thumb war because you will be way too busy concentrating on trying not to pee in your pants.

6. Bring apple juice.

Because when you finally arrive at Camp Win-Kee-Noo and are getting off the bus, it will make a lot more sense when you tell everyone that your pants were slightly wet from spilling apple juice on them and not because you really, really, really needed a bathroom.

7. Hold your breath inside an outhouse.

Because an outhouse is not really a house at all. It is a tiny bathroom with no plumbing, and it smells *so super stinky* that you'll have to pinch your nose and breathe through your mouth. And you'll think that maybe they should've named this place Camp Stink-Kee-Poo instead.

8. Bring toilet paper.

For obvious reasons.

9. Be the first one in the bunkhouse.

Because if you're last, then everyone will have already taken all the awesome top bunks, and you'll be stuck with a crummy bottom bunk underneath Luca "Butt Bazooka" Bambini, whose nickname says it all. And you'll wish your mom had packed a gas mask in your overnight bag.

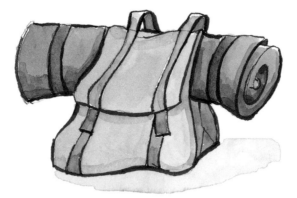

10. Pack your overnight bag yourself.

Because if you don't, your mom will, and even though she'll remember stuff like emergency snacks (Swamper-doodle cookies) and extra underwear, she will have forgotten to get a new sleeping bag to replace the one you ruined last Halloween.

Mom's good scissors that I'm not supposed to use

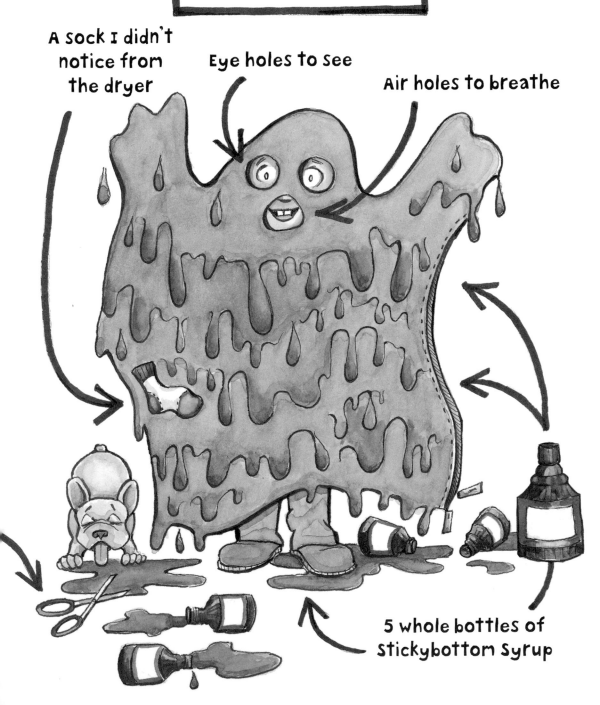

So instead she'll pack your big sister Winnie's sleeping bag, which is purple and has a glittery cupcake on it that says "Sweet Dreams." Then Kirby will point and laugh and say his baby sister has the same one.

11. If you spot a caterpillar, keep quiet about it.

Because if you point out the one that's crawling across the picnic table, Abner will pick it up before you can and run over to his mother yelling "Curious Creature!" And even though it's just a dumb old caterpillar, Mrs. V. will looked very pleased and nod and pat him on the head. Then she'll make a star next to Abner's name on her clipboard and pair up the rest of the troop to look for Curious Creatures too.

12. Try not to get stuck with a stinky partner.

Because being paired up with Luca will stink. Literally. And you'll have to pinch your nose every time he laughs and yells, "Fire in the hole!" And when you tell him you're never going to find Bigfoot if he keeps dropping booty bombs, Luca will say that you're never going to find him because he doesn't exist. That's when you'll head off in the opposite direction to look for Bigfoot on your own . . . and also because you'll really want some fresh air.

14. Avoid standing in patches of shiny green leaves.

Because they could end up being poison ivy, which will make your legs so itchy that you'll scratch (and scratch and scratch) until they turn all puffy and red. Then when you finally find your way back, Mrs. V. will send you straight to the camp doctor, who will put loads of pink, chalky lotion on your legs. And you will feel a million, billion times better.

But then you'll rejoin the troop and Abner will ask you too loudly why you're wearing his mom's pink knee socks.

15. Grip your canoe paddles tightly.

Because they can get pretty slippery when you're having an epic Swamp Scout SPLASHDOWN with Louie, and he might accidentally drop his paddle into the water. And when you try to help get his paddle back, you might accidentally lose yours too. Then you'll both be stuck in the middle of the lake with no way to steer back to shore, and you'll think things couldn't possibly get any worse.

16. Be prepared for the worst.

Because you and Louie will end up floating all the way across the lake to Camp Koo-Ka-Choo before being rescued by a bunch of *girls* from the Buttercup Brigade. Then you and Louie will have to listen to them chant:

BUTTERCUPS RULE!

the whole way back across the lake. And if that wasn't bad enough, Peggy Pinkerton, who's totally in love with you, will keep suggesting that maybe you need mouth-to-mouth even though you never fell into the water.

17. Don't believe everything you hear about pineapples.

Because Mrs. V. doesn't allow Abner to have any sweets, so she will try to convince him that the pineapple chunks she brought for him will be "just as tasty" as the marshmallows that everyone else is having, but you won't believe it because roasted marshmallows turn all gooey and melty and taste super delicious while roasted pineapples just turn black and shriveled and probably taste super burnt. And judging by the look on Abner's face, you'll bet you were right.

18. Sit as far away from Mrs. V. as possible.

Because Mrs. V. wears tons of perfume and tons of perfume attract tons of mosquitoes. And when you offer her your bug repellent, Kirby will grab it and spray it all over you and then complain that it doesn't work on "giant pests" because you haven't disappeared. And everyone will laugh and you'll decide to definitely add Kirby's name under Abner's in the "Terrible Things to Avoid" section of your Swamp Scout survival guide.

TERRIBLE THINGS TO AVOID

Hornets' nEST

The outhouse

The bottom bunk

Peggy Pinkerton

Snapping turtles
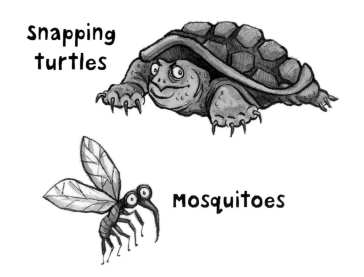

Mosquitoes

Abner

Rabbit poop

Poison ivy

Rubbery hot dogs

Kirby

Spiders

Roasted pineapple chunks

Being downwind
from Luca

19. Eat your emergency snacks quietly.

Because if you and Louie crunch too loudly, Abner will notice and say in his know-it-all way that you shouldn't eat sweets before bed, *especially* if you've already brushed your teeth. And you will say that it's not a problem because you have no intention of brushing your teeth OR going to bed.

And when he asks why, you'll tell him you plan to stay up all night and wait for Bigfoot to finally show up, which he definitely will, because you and Louie left some delicious Swamper-doodle cookies outside as bait.

20. Keep your eyes open
if you want to stay awake.

Because after a while, your eyelids will start to feel super heavy and you'll think you can close them for just a *teensy weensy bit*, but you will end up dozing off. And the next thing you know, Louie will be shaking you because he heard crunching sounds outside the bunkhouse. Then Luca will look kind of wide-eyed and panicked because he heard it too, and Kirby will dare you to go see what it is.

That's when Louie will give you that worried look he gives right before you're about to do something that maybe you shouldn't do.

THINGS I MAYBE
SHOULDN'T HAVE DONE

Flushing my
homework down
the toilet

Drawing on my face
with permanent marker
to stay home sick

Using Mom's fancy earring
as a fishing lure

Pouring hot sauce
on my tongue

Reading my big sister
Winnie's Diary

Trying out Grandpa's
teeth on the dog

But you'll be too excited to think things over, so you'll tell Louie to grab his camera and follow you outside.

Sweet Dreams

21. Get ready for greatness.

Because when you throw Winnie's sleeping bag over the shadowy figure that's crouched outside the bunkhouse crunching on cookies, it will wiggle and whimper and fall over in a heap. Then you'll yell "GOTCHA!" and tell Louie to get his camera ready because on the count of three you're going to pull off the sleeping bag and prove to everyone that Bigfoot is totally 100 percent real, just like you said.

22. Be prepared to make a startling discovery.

Because Swamper-doodle cookies could also attract something unexpected and totally terrible—like Abner Vanderpelt! And to makes things worse, he will have eaten *all of your cookies!* And when you say you're going to tell, he'll start to cry and beg you not to because his mom never lets him have any sweets.

Abner will say he was only going to try one, but they were so delicious that before he knew it he'd eaten them all. And you'll almost feel bad for him because he'll be crying so hard that chocolate and cookie crumbs will be streaming down his cheeks, making him look an awful lot like a giant, melting Swamper-doodle.

23. Avoid Abner
(especially if he looks like a giant, melting Swamper-doodle) at night in the woods.

Because he might be mistaken for Bigfoot bait. And the next thing you know, something big and furry will bumble its way through the bushes and head straight for you! Then Luca will yell "IT'S BIGFOOT!"

And Kirby will scream "HE'S REAL!" and everyone will scatter and run back to the bunkhouse, except for Abner because he's still too tangled up in your big sister's sleeping bag to move. Then you'll try hard to remember what to do if you ever come face-to-face with Bigfoot, but it'll be impossible to think with Abner clinging to you and wailing "DON'T EAT ME!"

24. Stay calm and everything will be OK.

Because Bigfoot doesn't eat Swamp Scouts (even if they're covered in chocolate). And he doesn't wear a pink, fuzzy bathrobe or curlers in his hair either. And he definitely doesn't stand with his hands on his hips and demand to know "What in blue blazes are you doing out of bed?"

But Mrs. V. does! And she'll look at you like maybe this whole thing was *your* idea, but before you can explain, Abner will already be making up a story about how he tripped in the dark on his way to the out-house and fell face-first into the mud. Then the angry line between Mrs. V.'s eyebrows will soften, and she'll say, "Oh, my poor, *poor darling*!" and she'll kiss the top of his head too many times. And you'll roll your eyes and bet no one else's mom would ever be so totally embarrassing.

25. If you don't have anything nice to say, don't say anything at all.

Because in the morning you'll wind up sitting next to Abner while his mom hands out the merit patches, and you'll have to watch *him* get the Curious Creature patch just for spotting that dumb old caterpillar. And you'll be so annoyed that you'll wish there was a Cookie-Crunching Crybaby patch so you could raise your hand and nominate Abner for being the biggest one . . . but you won't.

26. Remember that a cookie-crunching crybaby could surprise you.

Because when Mrs. V. says it's time to nominate someone to be this year's Steadfast Scout and that it must be awarded to someone who's brave and true and never gives up, Abner will raise his hand *as usual*. And just when you think he's going to nominate himself . . .

he will nominate *you* instead and say it's because you never stopped believing in Bigfoot. Then Luca and Kirby will raise their hands to add that you were super brave and Louie will say you're a true friend. Then Mrs. V. will *finally* call your name, and you'll feel like a giant roasted marshmallow that turned all gooey and melty on the inside.

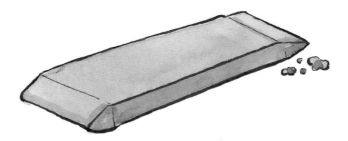

27. Bring an eraser.

Because you'll probably want to erase Abner's name from the "Terrible Things to Avoid" section of your Swamp Scout survival guide since he's not totally terrible *all the time.* And even though you didn't get a Curious Creature patch or prove to everyone that Bigfoot is real, you still wound up with an awesome merit patch anyway, which means now you have four! OK, fine, you only have three—the yellow one is still just a mustard stain.